he Lydia
Steptoe
Stories

Faber
Stories

Djuna Barnes was born in 1892 in Cornwall-on-Hudson in New York State. In 1912 she enrolled as a student at Pratt Institute and then at the Art Students' League, and while she was there she started to work as a reporter and illustrator for the *Brooklyn Eagle*. In 1921 she moved to Paris, where she lived for almost twenty years and wrote for such publications as *Vanity Fair* and *The New Yorker*. *Nightwood*, written in 1936, was her second novel. It is now considered a masterpiece, praised by T. S. Eliot for its 'great achievement of a style, the beauty of phrasing, the brilliance of wit and characterization, and a quality of horror and doom very nearly related to that of Elizabethan tragedy'. Her other works include *A Book*, a collection of short stories, poems and one-act plays; a satirical novel, *Ladies Almanack*; and a verse play, *The Antiphon*. She died in New York in 1982.

Djuna
Barnes

The Lydia
Steptoe
Stories

Faber
Stories

ff

First published in this single edition in 2019
by Faber & Faber Limited
Bloomsbury House
74–77 Great Russell Street
London WC1B 3DA

'The Diary of a Dangerous Child' first published in *Vanity Fair*, 1922
'The Diary of a Small Boy' first published in *Shadowland*, 1923
'Madame Grows Older: A Journal at the Dangerous Age' first published
in *Chicago Tribune Sunday Magazine*, 1924

Typeset by Faber & Faber Limited
Printed and bound by CPI Group (UK) Ltd, Croydon, CR0 4YY

A CIP record for this book
is available from the British Library

ISBN 978-0–571–35247–0

10 9 8 7 6 5 4 3 2 1

Djuna Barnes, the renowned author of the modernist novel *Nightwood*, wrote three short stories under the pseudonym 'Lydia Steptoe'. They appeared in different periodicals over three consecutive years in the 1920s; this is the first time they have been brought together as a set.

All written in ironic diary form, the Steptoe stories show Barnes at her wittiest and least self-consciously 'literary', a full decade before *Nightwood* was edited by T. S. Eliot and published by Faber.

The Diary of a Dangerous Child

September first:

Today I am fourteen: time flies: women must grow old.

Today I have done my hair in a different way and asked myself a question: "What shall be my destiny?"

Because today I have placed my childhood behind me, and have faced the realities.

My uncle from Glasgow, with the square whiskers and the dull voice, is bringing pheasants for my mother. I shall sit in silence during the meal and think. Perhaps someone, sensitive to growth, will ask in a tense voice, "What makes you look thoughtful, Olga?"

If this should be the case, I shall tell.

Yes, I shall break the silence.

For sooner or later they must know that I am become furtive.

By this I mean that I am debating with myself whether I shall place myself in some good man's hands and become a mother, or if I shall become wanton and go out in the world and make a place for myself.

Somehow I think I shall become a wanton.

It is more to my taste. At least I think it is.

I have tried to curb this inner knowledge by fighting down that bright look in my eyes as I stand before the mirror, but not ten minutes later I have been cutting into lemons for my freckles.

"Ah woman, thy name, etc."—

September third:

I could not write in my diary yesterday, my hands trembled and I started at every little thing. I think this shows that I am going to be anemic just as soon as I'm old enough to afford it.

This is a good thing; I shall get what I want. Yes, I am glad that I tremble early. Perhaps I am getting introspective. One must not look inward too much, while the inside is yet tender. I do not wish to frighten myself until I can stand it.

I shall think more about this tonight when mother puts the light out and I can eat a cream slowly. Some of my best thoughts have come to me this way.

Ah! What ideas have I not had eating creams slowly, luxuriously.

September tenth:

Many days have passed; I have written nothing. Can it be that I have changed? I will hold this thought solitary for a day.

September eleventh:

Yes, I have changed. I found that I owed it to the family.

I will explain myself. Father is a lawyer; mother is in society.

Imagine how it might look to the outer world if I should go around looking as if I held a secret.

If the human eye were to fall upon this page I might be so easily misunderstood.

What shame I might bring down upon my father's head—on my mother's too, if you want to take the whole matter in a large sweeping way—just by my tendency to precocity.

I should be an idiot for their sakes.

I will be!

October fourth:

I have succeeded. No one guesses that my mind teems. No one suspects that I have come into my own, as they say.

But I have. I came into it this afternoon when the diplomat from Brazil called.

My childhood is but a memory.

His name is Don Pasos Dilemma. He has great intelligence in one eye; the other is preoccupied with a monocle. He has comfortable spaces between his front teeth, and he talks in a soft drawl that makes one want to wear satin dresses.

He is courting my sister.

My sister is an extremely ordinary girl, older than I, it is true, but her spirit has no access to those things that I almost stumble over. She is not bad looking, but it is a vulgar beauty compared to mine.

There is something timeless about me, whereas my sister is utterly ephemeral.

I was sitting behind the victrola when he came in. I was reading *Three Lives*. Of course, he did not see me.

Alas for him, poor fellow!

My sister was there too; she kept walking up and down in the smallest sort of space, twisting her fan. He must have kissed her because she said, "Oh," and then he must have kissed her more intensely, because she said, "Oh," again, and drew her breath in, and in a moment she said softly, "You are a dangerous man!"

With that I sprang up and said in a loud and firm voice:

"Hurrah, I love danger!"

But nobody understood me.

I am to be put to bed on bread and milk.

Never mind, my room in which I sleep overlooks the garden.

October seventh:

I have been too excited to make any entry in my diary for a few days. Everything has been going splendidly.

I have succeeded in becoming subterranean. I have done something delightfully underhand. I bribed the butler to give a note to Don Pasos Dilemma, and I've frightened the groom into placing at my disposal a saddled horse. And I have a silver handled whip under my bed.

God help all men!

This is what I intend to do. I am going to meet Don Pasos Dilemma at midnight at the end of the arbor, and give him a whipping. For two reasons: one, because he deserves it, second, because it is Russian. After this I shall wash my hands of him, but the psychology of the family will have been raised one whole tone.

I'm sure of this.

Yes, at the full of the moon, Don Pasos Dilemma will be expecting me. His evil mind has already pictured me falling into his arms, a melting bit of tender and green youth.

Instead he will have a virago on his hands! How that word makes me shiver. There's only one other word that affects me as strongly—Vixen! These are my words!

Oh to be a virago at fourteen! What other woman has accomplished it?

No woman.

October eighth:

Last night arrived. But let me tell it as it happened.

The moon rose at a very early hour and hung, a great cycle in the heavens. Its light fell upon the laburnum bushes and lemon trees and gave me a sense of ice up and down my spine. I thought thoughts of Duse and how she had suffered on balconies a good deal; at least I gathered that she did from most of her pictures.

I too stood on the balcony and suffered side-face. The silver light glided over the smooth balustrade and swam in the pool of gold fishes.

In one hand I held the silver mounted whip. On my head was a modish, glazed riding hat with a single loose feather, falling sideways.

I could hear the tiny enamel clock on my ivory mantle ticking away the minutes. I began striking the welt of my riding boot softly. A high-strung woman must remember her duties to the malicious. I bit my under lip and thought of what I had yet to do. I leaned over the balcony and looked into the garden. There stood the stable boy in his red flannel shirt and beside him the fiery mare.

I tried to become agitated, my bosom refused to heave. Perhaps I am too young.

I shall leap from the balcony onto the horse's back. I whistled to the boy, he looked up, nodding. In a moment the mare was beneath my window. I looked at my wrist watch, it lacked two minutes to twelve. I jumped.

I must have miscalculated the shortness of the distance, or the horse must have moved. I landed in the stable boy's arms.

Oh well, from stable boy to prince, such has been the route of all fascinating women.

I struck my heels into the horse's side and was gone like the wind.

I can feel it yet—the night air on my cheeks, the straining of the great beast's muscles, the smell of autumn, the gloom, the silence. My own transcendent nature—I was coming to the man I hated—hated with a household hate. He who had kissed my sister, he who had never given me a second thought until this evening, and yet who was now all eagerness,—yes counting the minutes with thick, wicked, middle-aged poundings of a Southern heart.

When one is standing between life and death (any moment might have been my last), they say one reviews one's whole childhood. One's mind is said to go back over every little detail.

Anyway mine went back. The distance being so short it went back and forth.

I thought of the many happy hours I had spent with my youngest sister putting spiders down her back, pulling her hair, and making her eat my crusts. I thought of the hours I had lain in the dust beneath the sofa reading Petronius and Rousseau and Glyn. I thought of my father, a great, grim fellow standing six feet two in his socks, but mostly sitting in the Morris chair. Then I remembered the day I was fourteen, only a little over a month ago.

How old one becomes, and how suddenly!

I grew old on horseback, between twelve and twelve one.

For at twelve one precisely, I saw the form of Don Pasos Dilemma in the shadow of the trees, and my heart stopped beating, and I could feel all the childish uncertainties I had suffered become hard and firm, and I knew that I should never again be a child.

I could scarcely see how the betrayer was dressed, but I sensed that he had tricked himself out for the occasion. Had I been challenged, I should have wagered that he had perfumed himself behind the ears and under the chin. That's the kind of trick those foreign men are always up to.

I read that somewhere in a book.

Such men plan downfalls; they are so to speak connoisseurs of treachery; they are the virtuosi of viciousness.

I drew rein on the full four strokes of my horse's hoofs; I raised my silver mounted whip. I threw back my head. A laugh rang out in the stillness of midnight.

It was my laugh, high, drenched with the scorn of life and love and men.

It was a good laugh.

I brought the whip down—

October twenty-seventh:

I have changed my mind.

Yes, I have quite changed my mind. I am neither going to give myself into the hands of some good man, and become a mother, nor am I going to go out into the world and become a wanton. I am going to run away and become a boy.

For this Spaniard, this Brazilian, this Don

Pasos Dilemma scorned my challenge, the fine haughty challenge of a girl of youth and vigor, he scorned it, and cringing behind my mother, as it were, left me to face disillusion and chagrin at a late hour at night, when no nice girl should be out, much less facing anything.

For as you may have guessed, it was not Don Pasos who rode to meet me, it was my mother, wearing his long Spanish cloak.

November third:

In another year I shall be fifteen, a woman must grow young again. I have cut off my hair and I am asking myself nothing.

Absolutely nothing.

The Diary of a Small Boy

August seventh:

I am fourteen years old. I wear long trousers and stiff collars and I no longer turn around in the road to see if I am being watched. Nevertheless, I am told that I am not old enough to make any important observations.

I may not be old enough to put what I feel politely, but I feel what I feel, even if it is unpopular.

One of my most unpopular feelings, for instance, is Cousin Elda. She is a tall, obnoxious woman in her twenties, with great coarse, blonde braids. She comes from a far country— England or one of the Rhine towns, I forget which; and there she leaned out of a window a long time, watching the swift-running water on its way to the sea, or she said she did. I guess it's true, because she has a water-watching look, and she smiles all funny and interwoven and quiet.

She is not the only unnecessary woman around our place. There are my mother's two sisters, Clovine and Cresseda. They are insufficient as friends and practically evaporated as relatives.

They are little and whispering, and they are always making you nervous by the number of things they put their hands on. I wouldn't mind if they really wanted the things, or if they would only keep hold of them when then have got them. But they never do. They are always dropping them, and they are awfully sure about criminal law and how much punishment men should get.

They sit for hours talking of ways to make

bad men sorry. Sometimes I see them from afar off, dropping their knitting and working themselves up.

Sometime I'm going to think up a brand-new crime and see what they suggest.

I think my mother is not very partial to them. She always goes by them without stopping, even when she is talking to them, and if she has much to say, she goes by three or four times.

I have a little sister, but she is beside the point—she is only old enough to see people's good sides. I'm a little cool to her because she is eternally falling down and grinning about it in a way that proves her immature.

I'm going to leave her out of this diary because she is too young to resent it.

But wait until I get thru with the rest of them!

August tenth:

I have not taken my pen in hand for many days because I have been harassed.

There have been lots of people at our house, with many different ways, and it has taken me a long time to make up an idea of each of them.

But I'm settled about it now.

Yesterday there was a hunting party, and all the dogs and horses assembled on the green, down the driveway, and my mother came out of the house wearing a smart little riding-habit, and swinging a small whip in tiny, dangerous circles.

My father was there holding a gun at his side, and he kept patting it and looking it over, and locking it into second, or half-cock as it is called, and he looked very grand and handsome and superior to accident.

He has always been a very important man, but yesterday he claimed it.

My father is very great. He has dominating whiskers cut square for strength, and thinned out for delicacy. He wears quite a lot of rings because he is vain of his hands.

Usually one of his hands is between the leaves of some important book. Yesterday it was *War and Peace* and this morning it was *The Life of a Volupté*, whatever kind of life that is. But I like his hands best when he is cleaning his guns, or mending a saddle, or stroking the dogs.

He is broad-minded. He takes in all human aspects.

I wonder when I'm going to be a human aspect?

Anyway, they all went off, my cousin Elda looking every inch a woman in a riding-habit of gray and black.

She rode beside my father, and my mother went on in front without turning her head.

August twelfth:

I've been silent these past two days because I could not think up a name that was both beautiful enough, and strong enough to describe my mother.

If I say she is perilous, you get the feeling of trumpets and wars, and men riding down to doom. (Why is doom always down, and never up?) And if I say she is rare, you'll get an idea that she hardly ever comes down for breakfast and that she is inarticulate, and that won't do at all. If I say she is stupendous, you'll think that she must be over six feet tall, that she speaks in a loud voice, demands Shaw at the theaters, and expects strength from men and implacable democracy from women. All these impressions would be wrong.

She is small and dark and there is a hard softness about the place you put your head when you lean on her. She says "Dear" in a tone that makes you want to keep it away from everyone else.

She wears more rings than father, and her hands are kind, but they hurt if she wants them to. She wears loose clinging dresses, she walks in the garden with a hidden anger, and she cuts flowers for the house as if she were displeased, but all the time there is a smile in her face that makes you wait for something grand and terrible to occur.

August sixteenth:

I talked to the stable boy this morning. It seems to me that he is not so easy with me as he used to be. I must be growing up. Something is taking place in me.

I no longer feel dislike for my cousin Elda.

August eighteenth:

Today I walked about the outhouses and went down to examine the pump. I saw Elda coming around from the lilac bushes, smiling out of her large ox-eyes, the two braids falling down, one in front and one in back, and she was singing and walking slow.

She stopped a step or two away from me and said nothing for a minute, and then she asked me if I would like to go to the woods with her to gather wild flowers, and I said no, and she answered, "No?" in the same way I said it, only it sounded more hopeful.

She put her arm around me and said "No?" again, and I felt all disintegrated then she said, "Wouldn't you like to be a brave boy and go with me to protect me from the water snakes?"

Then that made me think of my father, and how safe it was for a long way all around him, when he held his gun that way in his hands, and patted it or cocked it, or just swung it down beside his leg with a careless air, and I said suddenly that I would go if I had a gun, but that I would not go otherwise.

She laughed and said, "Very well, I know where there is a beauty, and if you'll go with me I'll get it for you, but you must not tell, because you are your mother's darling and hope, and," she added suddenly, leaning down and looking into my face, "you are the link that binds them together, forever and ever." And I said I guessed so, and I felt all hot and excited and fearless.

She went away then to the house, and I stood by the trough dipping my hand in, so anyone seeing me would think me careless and occupied and would not question me.

The stable boy went by. "Growing up, kid?" he said, but I did not answer him. Presently she came out of the house carrying a basket on her arm. She came up to me and I looked in it and there lay one of father's South American pistols—one he had used when he was in charge of one of the more important of the canals; the pistol with the dull, dangerous, smoldering look of passion. And then we walked toward the woods saying nothing.

Presently she gave me the pistol. "Now remember, be careful, and shoot only if there is danger."

She went on ahead of me, singing under her breath, the two braids thrown back where I could see them, going down, down beyond the place for braids.

Presently she began turning the moss over with a stick and picking up things, green and damp and pretty, but nameless. The swamp water was black and thick. She went nearer and nearer, holding her blue dress up about her ankles, stepping over the black, wet stones—her feet kept sinking in, and she moved them softly and quickly. The skunk-cabbages were standing up out of the swamp angrily, all colored a boastful green.

"Do you love your mother?" she asked soon, and I answered:

"Yes. My father is a great man—"

She said: "Do you want to grow up some day like your father, and marry a beautiful woman and have a son to tie you together forever and forever, so no other beautiful woman can tear you apart?"

I said: "No beautiful woman could make me lose my head."

She laughed right out loud and stood up, looking at me, and said: "You are a baby— younger than I had imagined—"

"I'm old when I'm alone."

Then somehow, all of a sudden, everything got tangled up. She turned her head toward the swamp, screamed and slipped, and I saw a little water snake leaning over a rock, turning his tail around in a curl, and I saw the two yellow braids bent and funny and not straight as they always were and she fell against me, the gun went off, and the snake disappeared and I heard people shouting and running and my mother's voice high above everything: "Now she is trying those tricks on your son!" And her face was over me, looking as if the something terrible and tremendous that I had been waiting for, had happened— then I forgot—

October second:

We are not going to have hunting parties anymore. My father has put away all the guns and he sits on the porch for hours staring at the sun. My mother walks in the garden cutting flowers for the house.

Cousin Elda is gone. I guess she is leaning out of her window again, watching the water on its way to the sea.

I am not going to write any more in my diary, it is a girl's pastime—besides it hurts the wound in my side.

P. S. My mother's sisters talk more than ever about punishment for men—and it seems to be some man near the house here.

Madame Grows Older:
A Journal at the Dangerous Age

September seventh:

I must face the fact that I am no longer a young woman. I am a widow, mother of two thoroughly dressed, handsomely educated, spiteful daughters. Nevertheless I am starved. I am starved for youth. There must be, I tell myself, new worlds to conquer; there simply must be. It's only right.

When I was a child, and had curls down my back, I realized that it was horrible to be a child. Now that I am a matron, I realize that its horrible to be a matron. But I must not admit it, even to myself, I'm *so* volatile. In this year alone I've read *Frühlings Erwachen, A Night in the Luxembourg* and *Salomé* in

Greek. Successively I've burned, buried and mutilated them, but their message flames in my soul, only I can't read the message until the fire burns down. I must have patience.

September eighth:

I am about to confess in a big way. This is my confession. I have an unsatisfied, insubordinate gland somewhere about me, the same identical gland, I'm convinced, that produced the *Blue Bird* and gave that determined look of cheerfulness to the Hapsburgs. I think it is called the infantile gland; any way, there it is. It must have its day.

September ninth:

I have been all around the border of my lake. Leaning down I drew ever so many water lilies to me, crushing them against my heart—but my better nature bid me let them go. Then I gathered a handful of gravel and started tossing it at the goldfish, until it dawned upon me that I was satisfying an impulse to cruelty in a small way. Now I am resting under the sun-dial trying to calm my riotous nerves. As I sit I toy with a fallen maple leaf. Life and the seasons are so implacable, aren't they? They are here today and gone tomorrow, it's so splendid and heartless!

My God, as I sit here I realize that I am perishable! O if that brute of an Einstein had only taken a fancy to my relativity! Time and space are my enemies. If it were not for time,

I should not be dangerous, and if it were not for space, I should not feel so limited! How cruel is reason! How sharper than a serpent's tooth is meditation! How subtle is the lack of reason!

September tenth:

I said that I had made what was possibly my greatest confession. I lied! This is it: I am a girl, a mere child, amid my years. I have a sweet, forgiving nature, and I long to exert it, the trouble is that I've forgiven everything and everybody three or four times. I want to exert my womanly impulses, but there are so many womenly women exerting theirs, what chance have I who am no longer what I was?

On the other hand, of course, I have my feline qualities. I long to stretch out, at full length, on a couch, and hear men moaning about the corridors because I am indisposed. Ah how charming! I yearn to take up art. I feel, with my natural untrained instinct, I could mean a great deal to some new movement if I could only get it before it had moved much.

Then I want to be a psychic. I think there are ever so many messages just lost in space, waiting for a friend. For instance, I get a number of undefined feelings in a single day. Only yesterday I was mute with a sense of impending doom. The sense, or the doom, I don't know which, ran right through me. It was colossal! Might it not have heralded something of import? Perhaps it meant that red shoes were giving way to green; perhaps it presaged new dimensions; perhaps it meant there will be no more war. How can one tell? And I *must* know. I'm that way.

September eleventh:

Today I went driving. I got down at the park and went among those strangely innocent children one always sees in parks, pulling the swans about by their tails, sticking pins into the fish, and sitting on dogs. My arms were full of Little Elsie books, and a few copies of the *Story of Mankind* for those who are interested in retaliation. But no one seemed to want them.

I had half a dozen of those little rubber balls on elastic that come back at you, no matter what you do. These were for children at the breast. I sat a long time by the duck pond watching my reflection in the water, thinking on the inhumanity of man.

I was about to reenter my carriage, still thinking it, when my attention was attracted by a very young man. He could not have been over twenty-five. He had that peculiar dazed expression seen on the faces of immigrants who have been stunned in a foreign country. He might have been a Russian, a Swede, a Pole, an Italian, a Frenchman, he might have been anything. I did not know. I got hurriedly into my carriage and, directing the coachman to the Shelborne for tea, kept my eyes firmly fixed on the middle of his back.

September twelfth:

Today I returned to the park. I came empty handed, to be free, untroubled. "Alice," I said, "be vibrant, you are still young, you love life. A woman is as young as she looks, a man as young as he feels." "Alice," I said, "be a man, pull yourself together. You still pulse with the eternal scheme of things. You know you do." But my pulse tires me!

September thirteenth:

I cannot leave the park alone. I have become passionately attached to it. I sit by the pond and my thoughts revert to the young man of a day or two back. He was so manly. The perfect gentleman, so experienced without having learned anything, so tender and yet so racial. I think he would make my daughter Mariann, a fate second to none. I must meet him socially.

September fourteenth:

The welfare of my daughter is close to me— he is sitting on the bench just opposite. He is reading something. Is it Lettish, Finnish, Swedish? How beautiful is uncertainty!

September fifteenth:

All is well. My brother Alex happened to know the young man. He had no sooner set eyes on him than he exclaimed: "As I live, Prendaville Jones!" Imagine my delight. Prendaville Jones! The name is alive with possibilities!

September seventeenth:

The whole family has met him. Mariann has lost her appetite, she avoids me. Can it be that her heart has learned that secret gesture called love?

September eighteenth:

I have made a perfectly ghastly discovery! Oh, I can't write it! It has sent me to bed where I now lie writing it. The ink has dried on my pen for the hundredth time. I cannot put pen to paper. I am wrapped up in arnica and my head is done up in towels. Near at hand are the smelling salts, the Social Register and a guide to Monte Carlo. I am not myself.

I light cigarette after cigarette, and cast them all into that space outside my window that I used to call nature. Now I will not recognize nature. I have turned the lights off and on twenty times trying to calm myself. In vain! I am a moral and physical menace to human nature. This is it: I am in love with Prendaville Jones! I, a woman of forty, know once again the anguish of spring, the torture of love! I sleep badly, I scorn food. The fires of jealousy leap through me. I thirst for my daughter's life! My own daughter! And now I know what I must do. I don't want youth. I don't want passion. I want those dear, dead days that I used to spend thinking of my lost youth, imagining I wanted it back. I want those long, pleasant, unproductive moments with my Elsie books and my water lilies. I want those hours spent in mild, unfertile thoughts of danger. I want those basking, middle-years among my beautifully worn out acquaintances. I long for rest and the non-eventful forties. I tell you, I want to be untroubled once more.

This is what I am going to do. At midnight, on the hour, I shall dress myself in my lace dressing gown, and, taking the paper weight with the picture of St. George driving out the

dragons on the reverse side, I shall go down
though the tall grasses, as a matron should,
who is encased in her implacable years, and
there, at the pond's edge, cast myself in. No
one shall know that I blossomed again at the
age of discretion.

For I cannot bear the return of youth. It's
too much, I am too tired. I shall kill myself!

September nineteenth:

I have killed myself!